MVFOL

Get Ready, Mama!

To Kiana and Gabriel who have the
best mama in the world.
– S.G.

For Grandma 'Popi' Lily
– A.L.

First published 2022

EK Books
an imprint of Exisle Publishing Pty Ltd
PO Box 864, Chatswood, NSW 2057, Australia
226 High Street, Dunedin, 9016, New Zealand
www.ekbooks.org

A CiP record for this book is available from the National Library
of Australia.

ISBN 978-1-922539-08-3

Designed by Mark Thacker
Typeset in Minya Nouvelle 17 on 24pt
Printed in China

This book uses paper sourced under ISO 14001 guidelines
from well-managed forests and other controlled sources.

10 9 8 7 6 5 4 3 2 1

Get Ready, Mama!

SHARON GILTROW & ARIELLE LI

When you see your mama
roll over and open her eyes,
announce, **'Get Ready, Mama!'**

She will ask, 'Five more minutes please?'

And ...

... pull the covers over her head.

Say, 'Rise and shine.'

Tickle her feet, until she slides out of bed.

Give your mama
her favourite clothes.

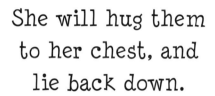

She will hug them
to her chest, and
lie back down.

Tell your mama,
'Quick, we're going
to be late.'

She will start crying
and reach for a cuddle.

Your mama is irresistible, and
you're never too late for cuddles.

Say, **'It's still time to get ready.'**

Watch as she puts her clothes on the wrong way.

Try not to laugh, and help her put them on the right way.

Then say, 'Breakfast time.'

Race your mama down the stairs.

Search for her
favourite cereal.

Empty!

Your mama will start to pout.

Quick, look in the fridge.

Give her ...

... whatever you can find.

Look at your mama,
look at your watch.

Tell her, 'Time to go.'

Grab your mama's bag
and start packing.

Say, 'Go get your shoes.'

Your mama will
stop to watch the TV.

Turn it off.

Your mama will stop to go to the potty.

Patiently wait ...

Some things can't be rushed.

Then, change your mama's top, because it has breakfast all over it.

As you are about to leave, your mama will come in, wearing her sparkly dance shoes.

Look at her, look at your watch.

Sigh!

Hand your mama her bag,
and bustle her out the door.

Turn around!

Scamper back into the house.

Shoo the puppy out the back door.

Lock the door!

Scurry to the car.

Remember ...
you can't drive.

Swap seats.

GRM-22

Look at your mama,

'Oh dear!'

Hand her 'The Get Your Mama Ready Pack'.

Watch as she ...

cleans her teeth,

brushes her hair,

puts on her make-up.

Then shout, **'DRIVE!!!'**

Scccrrreech ... into the carpark.

Oh no!

You're late!

Excuses you could use ...

'The puppy ate Mama's shoes.'

'Mama had to stop for a double skinny mama-cino.'

'Mama is late, because she's not on time.'

Kiss your mama goodbye.

Unwrap her arms from around your legs.

Give her one last hug.

Say, 'I'll see you later. Pinkie-promise.'

Give your mama a gentle nudge.

She will look at you with cutie eyes.

Slowly turn around, and ...

... RUN!